"Hay-ya!"

For Mom
With special thanks to Tiffany Stone

Text and illustrations © 2015 Chris Tougas

Owlkids Books acknowledges the financial support of the Canada Council for the Arts, the Ontario Arts Council, the Government of Canada through the Canada Book Fund (CBF) and the Government of Ontario through the Ontario Media Development Corporation's Book Initiative for our publishing activities.

Published in Canada by
Owlkids Books Inc.
10 Lower Spadina Avenue
Toronto, ON M5V 2Z2

Published in the United States by
Owlkids Books Inc.
1700 Fourth Street
Berkeley, CA 94710

Library and Archives Canada Cataloguing in Publication

Tougas, Chris, author, illustrator
        Dojo daytrip / Chris Tougas.

ISBN 978-1-77147-142-8 (bound)

        I. Title.

PS8589.O6774D653 2015   jC813'.54   C2014-908453-6

Library of Congress Control Number: 2015934526

The text is set in Bang Whack Pow.
Edited by: Karen Li
Designed by: Alisa Baldwin

Manufactured in Shenzhen, China, in March 2015, by C&C Joint Printing Co.
Job #H201500154R1A

A   B   C   D   E   F

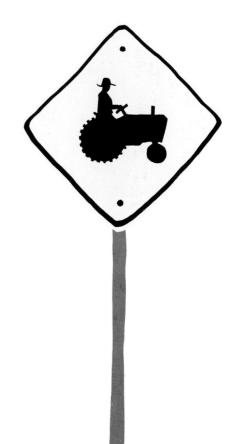

 Publisher of Chirp, chickaDEE and OWL
www.owlkidsbooks.com

DOJO DAYTRIP

Chris Tougas

Owlkids Books

The little ninjas shout, "Hooray!
Today's our Dojo Daytrip. Yay!"
With Master leading, arm in arm,
They leave the bus to tour the farm.

First they stop to feed the sow
When **suddenly**—

Master winds up in the trough,
While little ninjas scamper off—
Scaring scarecrows, freeing chicks,
Giving fences roundhouse kicks.

It's a big barnyard disaster!
No one's there to save the Master.
The ninjas all forgot their creed:
Always help someone in need.

Ninjas hide inside the barn,
As Master calls across the farm:
"Come and help me milk the cow!"
When **suddenly**—

Master flees the red barn, racing
From a bull that's charging, chasing.
Ninjas chase each other, too,
Making horns and yelling, *"Moo!"*

It's a big barnyard disaster!
No one's there to save the Master.
The ninjas all forgot their creed:
Always help someone in need.

Master hitches up the plow
When **suddenly**—

The horse is spooked and sprints away,
Dragging Master through the hay.

Ninjas clap and cheer him on
Until they realize...something's wrong!

It's a big barnyard disaster.
"SAVE ME, NINJAS!"
cries the Master.

Remembering their ninja creed,
They rush to help—with ninja speed!

With their Master safe and sound,
The little ninjas zip around.
They feed the sow, they milk the cow,
And give the field a ninja plow.

They fix things up around the farm—
And even paint the old, red barn!

The little ninjas give a bow.
Master bows and whispers...

Quietly, without fuss,
The ninjas board the ninja bus.

Ninjas sit down, row by row.
Master drives off nice and slow.
They sing their dojo travel song.
Master sighs and sings along.

All is calm—at least for now.
But down the road...